Jenny
AND THE
GRAND OLD GREAT-AUNTS

COLBY RODOWSKY

Jenny

AND THE

Bradbury Press / New York

Maxwell Macmillan Canada / Toronto
Maxwell Macmillan International
New York / Oxford / Singapore / Sydney

GRAND OLD GREAT-AUNTS

illustrated by Barbara J. Roman

Bradbury Press
Macmillan Publishing Company
866 Third Avenue
New York, NY 10022

Maxwell Macmillan Canada, Inc.
1200 Eglinton Avenue East
Suite 200
Don Mills, Ontario M3C 3N1

Macmillan Publishing Company is part of
the Maxwell Communication Group of Companies.

First edition
Printed and bound in the United States of America
1   2   3   4   5   6   7   8   9   10

The text of this book is set in 15 point Goudy Old Style.
The illustrations are rendered in color pencil and watercolor on
plate-finished Bristol paper.

LIBRARY OF CONGRESS CATALOGING-IN-PUBLICATION DATA
Rodowsky, Colby.
Jenny and the grand old great-aunts / by Colby Rodowsky. — 1st ed.
p.   cm.
Summary: Jenny's apprehension about spending an afternoon with
her two elderly great-aunts is forgotten when one of the aunts takes
her into the old attic.
ISBN 0-02-777785-5
[1. Great-aunts — Fiction.]   I. Roman, Barbara J., ill.
II. Title. PZ7.R7986Je   1992
[E] — dc20   90-42563

IT WAS A SATURDAY AFTERNOON, and Mama had to go to the dentist, and Papa had to drop by the office, and then after that they both had to stop and see a friend in the hospital. And they said, in a way that meant they'd already decided, that this would be a good day for Jenny to visit the aunts.

"By myself?" said Jenny, her voice sounding high and squeaky. "But I've never been to visit the aunts all by myself. Only with you and Mama. And besides, there's nothing to *do* there."

"There's everything to do there, I know for a fact," said Papa, taking the lunch dishes off the table and piling them into the sink. "Because when I was little and my parents had to go out, they always left me with Aunt Abby and Aunt Clare."

"What did you do?" said Jenny. She scrunched down low in her chair and looked at her father over the tops of her glasses.

"I used to swing on the lowest branch of the maple tree," said Papa, "and play pirate ship in the wheelbarrow. I used to dig for worms in the cabbage patch and pick beetles off the rose bushes."

"I can't do any of that," said Jenny, looking out at the gray winter sky and the snow covering the ground.

"And then there was the attic," said Papa. He filled the sink with water and added soap. He started to sing. "Great-aunts, old aunts. Grand old great-aunts."

"What about the attic?" said Jenny. But Papa was singing and washing and making mountains out of soap bubbles, and he didn't hear her.

"What about the attic?" whispered Jenny to herself. "What about the attic?"

Just then her mother came in carrying Jenny's favorite doll. She put it on the table. "You could take Miranda with you when you go to the aunts," said Mama. "That way you'll be sure to have something to do."

"I guess," said Jenny. She picked the doll up by one leg and knew, by the look on her face, that Miranda didn't want to go to visit the aunts any more than she did.

After the dishes were done, Jenny and her mother and father put on their coats and went outside. "Great-aunts, old aunts," sang Papa as they got in the car and drove up one street and down another.

"Grand old great-aunts," Mama joined in.

Jenny pressed her face flat against the windowpane and watched the world going by outside. She saw a poodle in a yellow coat and a boy pulling a sled. She saw an icicle as long as her arm. She chewed on the end of her mitten and thought secretly that *getting* to Aunt Clare and Aunt Abby's house was more fun than *being* there.

Aunt Clare and Aunt Abby were waiting
at the window when the car pulled up out
front. They opened the door and beckoned
for Jenny and her mother and father to come
inside.

11

"Before the heat gets out," said Aunt Clare in her high, flutey voice.

"Before the cold gets *in*," said Aunt Abby in her low, rumbly voice.

"Hello, hello," said Aunt Clare.

"We're glad to see you," said Aunt Abby. And then the aunts stood back and looked at Jenny for a very long time before they said, "She's getting to be a *big* girl."

Jenny held tight to Miranda and looked up at the aunts, thinking that they were just alike in their dark-colored dresses with their gray wispy hair. "Except that Aunt Clare is tall and Aunt Abby is short," she said to herself. Then Aunt Clare stepped forward and unzipped Jenny's coat with her long, bony fingers, and Aunt Abby hung it on the coatrack next to a green umbrella. And they all went single file into the parlor.

At Aunt Clare and Aunt Abby's house everything was neat and tidy and exactly the way that it had been when Jenny was there before. The blue glass slipper was still on the table by the window. The china elephant was still on the top of the bookcase. The window shades were still pulled halfway down. And the big orange cat was still asleep on the piano.

"A place for everything and everything
in its place," Aunt Clare said.

At Aunt Clare and Aunt Abby's house everybody spoke in whispers, and the clock ticked and tocked, and after a very long time it chimed, and after another long time it chimed again.

At Aunt Clare and Aunt Abby's house everyone kept his feet on the floor and his hands in his lap, only Jenny's feet didn't *reach* the floor and sometimes, between the ticking and the tocking of the clock, she heard Aunt Abby's fingers making drum noises on the underside of her chair.

Finally Mama stood up and said, "We'd better go so we can get back."

16

Papa stood up. "We won't be long."

Mama said, "Be a good girl, Jenny."

Papa said, looking at the aunts, "You're sure, now, that it's no bother?"

"Nonsense," said Aunt Clare.

"Remember how we took care of you when *you* were a little boy?" said Aunt Abby.

17

And for a minute Jenny closed her eyes and tried to think of Papa ever being a little boy. And when she opened them again and Papa asked if everything was okay, she said "Fine," even though this was the first time she'd stayed by herself with the aunts and she didn't feel fine at all and knew, deep down, that she'd rather go to the dentist and the office and to see the friend in the hospital. Then Papa waved and Mama blew a kiss, and they went through the hall and out the door, and Jenny was alone with Aunt Clare and Aunt Abby.

The three of them sat in
the parlor and listened to the
clock tick and the pipes make
clanging noises inside the
walls. Jenny picked at a Band-
Aid on her knee and twisted
around to count the books in
the bookcase. She stopped
when she got to one hundred
and thirty-seven. The cover
on the sofa scratched the
backs of her legs and she
moved over to a chair by the
window, holding Miranda up
so that she could dance along
the sill.

"Don't fidget, Jenny," said
Aunt Clare.

"Wiggle worm," said Aunt Abby. But the way she said it made a wiggle worm sound like it was the best possible kind of a worm to be.

"Wiggle worm," said Jenny under her breath. "Wiggle worm—wiggle worm—wiggle worm."

Aunt Clare sighed and picked up her knitting.

Jenny looked at the glass slipper and wondered if it would fit Miranda. She stared at the cat on the piano and wished that he would wake up and play with her. She watched the hands of the clock and tried to remember what time her mother and father had left and worried about when they would come back.

"What if they're gone a really long time and I have to go to the bathroom and I can't remember where it is?" thought Jenny.

21

"And what if they forget me and I have to stay forever?"

Jenny pulled Miranda close. She felt a lump growing in her throat and two tears running down her face.

Just then Aunt Abby leaned forward, touching the tip of Jenny's shoe and saying, "Are you all right, dear?"

"I guess," said Jenny. She sniffed and gulped and wiped her nose on the back of her hand.

"Oh dear," said Aunt Abby. "I did so want you to have a lovely time. She rocked back in her chair and thought for a minute.

"We could go outside and dig in the cabbage patch—except that it's too cold and the ground is frozen hard," she said. "We could play 'Chopsticks' on the piano except that Aunt Clare seems to have dozed off and I'd hate to wake her, not to mention the cat."

Jenny looked over and saw that Aunt Clare's eyes were closed and that her mouth made in and out huffing noises.

"Oh dear," said Aunt Abby again. Then all of a sudden she jumped up, clapping her hands and beckoning for Jenny to follow her.

And together the two of them took giant tiptoe steps out of the parlor and through the hall and up the stairs, past a row of portraits all looking straight ahead. They went along the second floor hall and through Aunt Clare's sewing room at the front of the house to a tall, white door.

Aunt Abby unlatched the door and opened it and went ahead, calling back over her shoulder for Jenny to mind the steps.

"Mind—the—steps," said Jenny as she climbed up, up, up into the attic.

The attic was hot and dry and smelled like the insides of pockets.

There were trunks and boots and books in piles. There were baskets hanging from the rafters and canes and curtain rods and fishing poles in a heap on the floor next to a broken-down rocking chair. There was a piano stool that got higher and then lower again when Jenny turned around on it, and a picture of a lion in a frame that looked like a cage, with bars across the front.

And there was something called a Victrola. Aunt Abby stood Jenny on an upside-down wooden box in front of it and put her hand on the handle and together they wound it tighter and tighter. Then Aunt Abby set the needle down on the record, and a funny, thin kind of music came out.

Aunt Abby opened one of the trunks under the rafters and took out a hat with a bird on it and put it on Jenny's head. Then she took out a long, puffy streamer all made of pink feathers.

"A boa," she said as she hung it around her shoulders.

"A boa," said Jenny, liking the way the word sounded on her tongue. "Boa—boa—boa," she said, just as the music stopped.

When Aunt Abby went to rewind the Victrola, the ends of the boa brushed against Jenny's face and felt like fingers made of feathers.

The music started again and Aunt Abby hitched the boa higher on her shoulders.

She nodded her head and her feet made little sideways steps on the floor.

She swung one arm and then the other and spun around so quickly Jenny wasn't sure she had done it at all.

She sailed across the clear middle part of the floor. She swooped and swayed and stamped her feet in time to the thin, funny music. She twirled the ends of the boa.

And when the music stopped she waited while Jenny climbed on the box and wound the Victrola and took the needle off and put it on again—all by herself.

Aunt Abby took Jenny's hand, and the two of them made sideways steps on the floor.

They swung their arms and spun around.

They sailed across the clear middle part of the floor, swooping and swaying and stamping their feet in time to the music.

They stopped to rest in front of a mirror that leaned against the wall. The mirror was blotchy and sort of magic. Nothing in it looked like it looked in real life.

Jenny found a stack of books on a table in the corner, and Aunt Abby said that they had been hers and Aunt Clare's when they were little girls. It was even harder to think of the aunts as little girls than it was to think of Papa as a little boy, thought Jenny. And she wondered if when Aunt Clare and Aunt Abby were little their hair was gray, the way it was now. She wondered if their skin had lines in it then.

"What did you do when *you* were a little girl?" asked Jenny. Aunt Abby answered right away, as if it has been just yesterday.

"Oh, we played," she said. "With games and dolls and India rubber balls."

And all of a sudden Aunt Abby dragged a chest out into the middle of the floor. She threw back the lid, rooted around inside, and pulled out a doll with yellow hair, a set of dishes, and a bank in the shape of a whale.

She pulled out a beanbag and a Noah's ark made of wood.

"Aha," she said as she sat on the floor, turning the ark upside down and spilling the animals out around her.

Then Jenny set Miranda down next to the doll with yellow hair, and she and Aunt Abby lined the animals up two by two.

They marched them in a grand parade around the side of the trunk and across the floor, along past the mirror, in and out of the shadows, and under the Victrola. They marched them up to the picture of a lion in a frame that looked like a cage and they roared at him.

The lion roared back.

After a while Jenny and Aunt Abby heard Aunt Clare calling from the first floor. "Yoo-hoo," she said. "Come along now for tea."

Aunt Abby looked at her watch and then at Jenny.

"Well, yes," she said. "We'd better hurry."

Aunt Abby and Jenny put the animals back in the ark. They put the ark and the doll, the tea set, the beanbag, and the bank in the shape of a whale back in the chest. They slid the chest under the rafters and closed the lid of the Victrola and turned the wooden box right side up. Jenny took off her hat and Aunt Abby took off her pink feather boa, and they laid them in the trunk.

They looked in the mirror one last time before Jenny picked up Miranda and they all went down the steps.

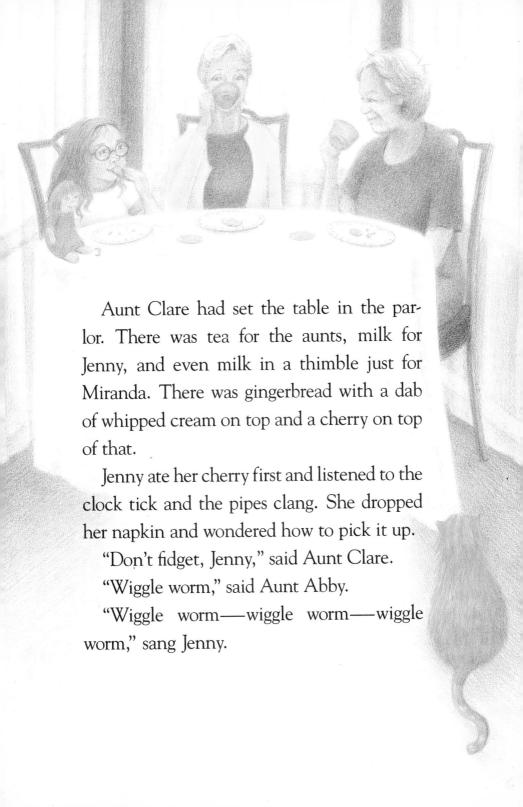

Aunt Clare had set the table in the parlor. There was tea for the aunts, milk for Jenny, and even milk in a thimble just for Miranda. There was gingerbread with a dab of whipped cream on top and a cherry on top of that.

Jenny ate her cherry first and listened to the clock tick and the pipes clang. She dropped her napkin and wondered how to pick it up.

"Don't fidget, Jenny," said Aunt Clare.

"Wiggle worm," said Aunt Abby.

"Wiggle worm—wiggle worm—wiggle worm," sang Jenny.

Mama and Papa came in, the cold outside air sticking to their clothes, and when they kissed Jenny their lips made icy patches on her cheek that turned warm before they finally wore away. Mama and Papa had tea and talked about the dentist and the office and the trip to visit the friend in the hospital. Then they stood up and said that it was time to go.

Aunt Abby got Jenny's coat from the coatrack in the hall. Aunt Clare zipped her up in it with her long, bony fingers.

"Thank you," said Jenny.

"You're welcome," said the aunts. "And come again."

"I will," said Jenny. "And Miranda will, too."

Then Mama and Papa and Jenny went down the walk. They turned at the end, waving back to Aunt Clare and Aunt Abby.

"I didn't want to say anything before," said Mama. "But did you notice that Aunt Abby had pink things in her hair?"

Papa wiggled his eyebrows and thought for a minute. He made a little lion noise in his throat. "Feathers," he said.

"Feathers?" said Mama.

"From a boa," said Papa.

"A boa?" said Mama.

"A boa," said Papa and Jenny both at the same time.

And they all joined hands and sang the "Great-aunts, old aunts, grand old great-aunts" song as they climbed into the car.